How's the Weather?

Acknowledgments
Executive Editor: Diane Sharpe
Supervising Editor: Stephanie Muller
Design Manager: Sharon Golden
Page Design: Simon Balley Design Associates
Photography: Bruce Coleman: pages 11, 17, 19, 21, 23, 29;
Chris Fairclough Colour Library: page 15; Oxford Scientific Films:
cover (right), pages 7, 13 (both); Tony Stone Worldwide: cover (left),
pages 9, 25.

ISBN 0-8114-3700-0

Copyright © 1995 Steck-Vaughn Company.

1 2 3 4 5 6 7 8 9 0 PO 00 99 98 97 96 95 94

How's the Weather?

Helen Barden

Illustrated by

Katy Sleight

STECK-VAUGHN
C O M P A N Y
ELEMENTARY • SECONDARY • ADULT • LIBRARY

If it rains I can...

splash in the puddles

or open up my umbrella.

Do you know that birds wash their feathers in the rain?

If it's windy I can...

play with my kite

or blow bubbles.

8

In autumn the wind blows the leaves off the trees.

If it's frosty I can...

break off the icicles

or slide on the ice.

Frost makes the spider's web sparkle.

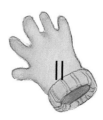

If it snows I can...

build a snowman

or play on my sled.

You can see animal tracks in the snow.

If it's stormy I can...

watch the lightning

and listen to the thunder.

14

Sheep huddle together in a storm.

If it's sunny I can...

play in my wading pool

and wear my shorts and T-shirt.

16

Butterflies visit the flowers in the sunshine.

I hope it's sunny.
Then I can...

work in the garden

and hang up the washing.

On sunny days you can hear the
bees buzzing.

If it's foggy I can...

play in the house

and watch TV.

You can't see things clearly in
the fog.

If there is a hurricane I can...

listen to the weather report

and look after my pets.

22

Nothing likes to be out in a hurricane.

If it's cloudy...

I won't know what to wear.

It could start to rain.

24

Or the sun could peek through
the clouds.

But it's sunny, too, so guess what I can see?

Which of these things would you need for rainy, sunny, frosty, snowy, or windy weather?

Index

Clouds **24-25**

Fog **20-21**
Frost **10-11**

Hurricane **22-23**

Lightning **14**

Rain **6-7, 24, 28**
Rainbow **29**

Snow **12-13**
Storm **14-15**
Sun **16-17, 18-19, 25**

Thunder **14**

Wind **8-9**